Ian Whybrow

Babies Can!

Illustrated by
Lara Jones

Macmillan Children's Books

Babies can't help . . .

Daisy

They can't
do buttons...

George

but they can undress.

They can't say "sheep"...

They can't say
"I'm hungry"...

but they can say
"Waaa!"

They can't
use spoons . . .

so this is how they eat.

They can't stay clean . . .

but they can look sweet.

Babies can't build . . .

but they can go

BASH!

Babies can't paddle . . .

but they can catch bugs.

They can't say
"I love you!"...

but they can do . . .

For King S, Jessie, and George – L.J.

For Ella Rose with love – I.W.

First published in 2005 by Macmillan Children's Books
A division of Macmillan Publishers Limited
20 New Wharf Road, London N1 9RR
Basingstoke and Oxford
Associated companies throughout the world
www.panmacmillan.com

ISBN 0 333 97361 5 HB
ISBN 0 333 97362 3 PB

1 3 5 7 9 8 6 4 2 HB
1 3 5 7 9 8 6 4 2 PB

A CIP catalogue record for this book is available from the British Library.

Printed in Belgium by Proost.